UNDER THE GARDEN

GRAHAM GREENE

UNDER THE GARDEN

penguin books

PENGUIN BOOKS

Published by the Penguin Group
Penguin Books USA Inc., 375 Hudson Street,
New York, New York 10014, U.S.A.
Penguin Books Ltd, 27 Wrights Lane,
London W8 5TZ, England
Penguin Books Australia Ltd, Ringwood,
Victoria, Australia
Penguin Books Canada Ltd, 10 Alcorn Avenue,
Toronto, Ontario, Canada M4V 3B2
Penguin Books (N.Z.) Ltd, 182–190 Wairau Road,
Auckland 10, New Zealand

Penguin Books Ltd, Registered Offices:
Harmondsworth, Middlesex, England

Published in Penguin Books 1995

"Under the Garden" was first published in Graham Greene's *A Sense of Reality* published by The Viking Press. It later appeared in *Collected Stories* by Graham Greene published in Penguin Books.

ISBN 0 14 60.0057 9

Printed in the United States of America

UNDER THE GARDEN

Part One

I

It was only when the doctor said to him, 'Of course the fact that you don't smoke is in your favour,' Wilditch realized what it was he had been trying to convey with such tact. Dr Cave had lined up along one wall a series of X-ray photographs, the whorls of which reminded the patient of those pictures of the earth's surface taken from a great height that he had pored over at one period during the war, trying to detect the tiny grey seed of a launching ramp.

Dr Cave had explained, 'I want you clearly to understand my problem.' It was very similar to an intelligence briefing of such 'top secret' importance that only one officer could be entrusted with the information. Wilditch felt gratified that the choice had fallen on him, and he tried to express his interest and enthusiasm, leaning forward and examining more closely than ever the photographs of his own interior.

'Beginning at this end,' Dr Cave said, 'let me see, April, May, June, three months ago, the scar left by the pneumonia is quite obvious. You can see it here.'

'Yes, sir,' Wilditch said absent-mindedly. Dr Cave gave him a puzzled look.

'Now if we leave out the intervening photographs for the moment and come straight to yesterday's, you will observe that this latest one is almost entirely clear, you can only just detect . . .'

'Good,' Wilditch said. The doctor's finger moved over what might have been tumuli or traces of prehistoric agriculture.

'But not entirely, I'm afraid. If you look now along the whole series you will notice how very slow the progress has been. Really by this stage the photographs should have shown no trace.'

'I'm sorry,' Wilditch said. A sense of guilt had taken the place of gratification.

'If we had looked at the last plate in isolation I would have said there was no cause for alarm.' The doctor tolled the last three words like a bell. Wilditch thought, is he suggesting tuberculosis?

'It's only in relation to the others, the slowness . . . it suggests the possibility of an obstruction.'

'Obstruction?'

'The chances are that it's nothing, nothing at all. Only I wouldn't be *quite* happy if I let you go without a deep examination. Not *quite* happy.' Dr Cave left the photographs and sat down behind his desk. The long pause seemed to Wilditch like an appeal to his friendship.

2   'Of course,' he said, 'if it would make you happy . . .'

It was then the doctor used those revealing words, 'Of course the fact that you don't smoke is in your favour.'

'Oh.'

'I think we'll ask Sir Nigel Sampson to make the examination. In case there is something there, we couldn't have a better surgeon . . . for the operation.'

Wilditch came down from Wimpole Street into Cavendish Square looking for a taxi. It was one of those summer days which he never remembered in childhood: grey and dripping. Taxis drew up outside the tall liver-coloured buildings partitioned by dentists and were immediately caught by the commissionaires for the victims released. Gusts of wind barely warmed by July drove the rain aslant across the blank eastern gaze of Epstein's virgin and dripped down the body of her fabulous son. 'But it hurt,' the child's voice said behind him. 'You make a fuss about nothing,' a mother – or a governess – replied.

2

This could not have been said of the examination Wilditch endured a week later, but he made no fuss at all, which perhaps aggravated his case in the eyes of the doctors who took his calm for lack of vitality. For the unprofessional to enter a hospital or to enter the services has very much the same effect; there is a sense of relief and indifference; one is placed quite helplessly on a conveyor-belt with no responsibility any more for anything. Wilditch felt himself protected by an organization, while the English summer dripped outside on the coupés of the parked cars. He had not felt such freedom since the war ended.

The examination was over – a bronchoscopy; and there remained a nightmare memory, which survived through the cloud of the anaesthetic, of a great truncheon forced down his throat into the chest and then slowly withdrawn; he woke next morning bruised and raw so that even the act of excretion was a pain. But that, the nurse told him, would pass in one day or two; now he could dress and go home. He was disappointed at the abruptness with which they were thrusting him off the belt into the world of choice again.

'Was everything satisfactory?' he asked, and saw from the nurse's expression that he had shown indecent curiosity.

'I couldn't say, I'm sure,' the nurse said. 'Sir Nigel will look in, in his own good time.'

Wilditch was sitting on the end of the bed tying his tie when Sir Nigel Sampson entered. It was the first time Wilditch had been conscious of seeing him: before he had been a voice addressing him politely out of sight as the anaesthetic took over. It was the beginning of the week-end and Sir Nigel was dressed for the country in an old tweed jacket. He had tousled white hair and he looked at

4

Wilditch with a far-away attention as though he were a float bobbing in midstream.

'Ah, feeling better,' Sir Nigel said incontrovertibly.

'Perhaps.'

'Not very agreeable,' Sir Nigel said, 'but you know we couldn't let you go, could we, without taking a look?'

'Did you see anything?'

Sir Nigel gave the impression of abruptly moving downstream to a quieter reach and casting his line again.

'Don't let me stop you dressing, my dear fellow.' He looked vaguely around the room before choosing a strictly upright chair, then lowered himself on to it as though it were a tuffet which might 'give'. He began feeling in one of his large pockets – for a sandwich?

'Any news for me?'

'I expect Dr Cave will be along in a few minutes. He was caught by a rather garrulous patient.' He drew a large silver watch out of his pocket – for some reason it was tangled up in a piece of string. 'Have to meet my wife at Liverpool Street. Are *you* married?'

'No.'

'Oh, well, one care the less. Children can be a great responsibility.'

'I have a child – but she lives a long way off.'

'A long way off? I see.'

'We haven't seen much of each other.'

'Doesn't care for England?'

'The colour-bar makes it difficult for her.' He realized how childish he sounded directly he had spoken, as though he had been trying to draw attention to himself by a bizarre confession, without even the satisfaction of success.

'Ah, yes,' Sir Nigel said. 'Any brothers or sisters? You, I mean.'

'An elder brother. Why?'

'Oh, well, I suppose it's all on the record,' Sir Nigel said, rolling in his line. He got up and made for the door. Wilditch sat on the bed with the tie over his knee. The door opened and Sir Nigel said, 'Ah, here's Dr Cave. Must run along now. I was just telling Mr Wilditch that I'll be seeing him again. You'll fix it, won't you?' and he was gone.

'Why should I see him again?' Wilditch asked and then, from Dr Cave's embarrassment, he saw the stupidity of the question. 'Oh, yes, of course, you did find something?'

'It's really very lucky. If caught in time . . .'

'There's sometimes hope?'

'Oh, there's always hope.'

So, after all, Wilditch thought, I am – if I so choose – on the conveyor-belt again.

Dr Cave took an engagement-book out of his pocket and said briskly, 'Sir Nigel has given me a few dates. The

tenth is difficult for the clinic, but the fifteenth – Sir

Nigel doesn't think we should delay longer than the fifteenth.'

'Is he a great fisherman?'

'Fisherman? Sir Nigel? I have no idea.' Dr Cave looked aggrieved, as though he were being shown an incorrect chart. 'Shall we say the fifteenth?'

'Perhaps I could tell you after the week-end. You see, I have not made up my mind to stay as long as that in England.'

'I'm afraid I haven't properly conveyed to you that this is serious, really serious. Your only chance – I repeat your only chance,' he spoke like a telegram, 'is to have the obstruction removed in time.'

'And then, I suppose, life can go on for a few more years.'

'It's impossible to guarantee . . . but there have been complete cures.'

'I don't want to appear dialectical,' Wilditch said, 'but I do have to decide, don't I, whether I want my particular kind of life prolonged.'

'It's the only one we have,' Dr Cave said.

'I see you are not a religious man – oh, please don't misunderstand me, nor am I. I have no curiosity at all about the future.'

The past was another matter. Wilditch remembered a leader in the Civil War who rode from an undecided battle mortally wounded. He revisited the house where he was born, the house in which he was married, greeted a few retainers who did not recognize his condition, seeing him only as a tired man upon a horse, and finally – but Wilditch could not recollect how the biography had ended: he saw only a figure of exhaustion slumped over the saddle, as he also took, like Sir Nigel Sampson, a train from Liverpool Street. At Colchester he changed on to the branch line to Winton, and suddenly summer began, the kind of summer he always remembered as one of the conditions of life at Winton. Days had become so much shorter since then. They no longer began at six in the morning before the world was awake.

Winton Hall had belonged, when Wilditch was a child, to his uncle, who had never married, and every summer he lent the house to Wilditch's mother. Winton Hall had been virtually Wilditch's, until school cut the period short, from late June to early September. In memory his mother and brother were shadowy background figures. They were less established even than the machine upon the platform of 'the halt' from which he bought Fry's chocolate for a penny a bar: than the oak tree spreading over the green in front of the red-brick wall – under its shade as a child he had distributed apples to soldiers halted there in the hot August of 1914: the group of silver birches on the Winton lawn and the broken fountain, green with slime. In his memory he did not share the house with others: he owned it.

Nevertheless the house had been left to his brother not to him; he was far away when his uncle died and he had never returned since. His brother married, had children (for them the fountain had been mended), the paddock behind the vegetable garden and the orchard, where he used to ride the donkey, had been sold (so his brother had written to him) for building council-houses, but the hall and the garden which he had so scrupulously remembered nothing could change.

Why then go back now and see it in other hands? Was it that at the approach of death one must get rid of everything? If he had accumulated money he would now have been in the mood to distribute it. Perhaps the man who had ridden the horse around the countryside had not been saying goodbye, as his biographer imagined, to what he valued most: he had been ridding himself of illusions by seeing them again with clear and moribund eyes, so that he might be quite bankrupt when death came. He had the will to possess at that absolute moment nothing but his wound.

His brother, Wilditch knew, would be faintly surprised by this visit. He had become accustomed to the fact that 9

Wilditch never came to Winton; they would meet at long intervals at his brother's club in London, for George was a widower by this time, living alone. He always talked to others of Wilditch as a man unhappy in the country, who needed a longer range and stranger people. It was lucky, he would indicate, that the house had been left to him, for Wilditch would probably have sold it in order to travel further. A restless man, never long in one place, no wife, no children, unless the rumours were true that in Africa ... or it might have been in the East ... Wilditch was well aware of how his brother spoke of him. His brother was the proud owner of the lawn, the goldfish-pond, the mended fountain, the laurel-path which they had known when they were children as the Dark Walk, the lake, the island ... Wilditch looked out at the flat hard East Anglian countryside, the meagre hedges and the stubbly grass, which had always seemed to him barren from the salt of Danish blood. All these years his brother had been in occupation, and yet he had no idea of what might lie underneath the garden.

4

The chocolate-machine had gone from Winton Halt, and the halt had been promoted – during the years of nationali-
zation – to a station; the chimneys of a cement-factory

smoked along the horizon and council-houses now stood three deep along the line.

Wilditch's brother waited in a Humber at the exit. Some familiar smell of coal-dust and varnish had gone from the waiting-room and it was a mere boy who took his ticket instead of a stooped and greying porter. In childhood nearly all the world is older than oneself.

'Hullo, George,' he said in remote greeting to the stranger at the wheel.

'How are things, William?' George asked as they ground on their way – it was part of his character as a countryman that he had never learnt how to drive a car well.

The long chalky slope of a small hill – the highest point before the Ural mountains he had once been told – led down to the village between the bristly hedges. On the left was an abandoned chalk-pit – it had been just as abandoned forty years ago, when he had climbed all over it looking for treasure, in the form of brown nuggets of iron pyrites which when broken showed an interior of starred silver.

'Do you remember hunting for treasure?'

'Treasure?' George said. 'Oh, you mean that iron stuff.'

Was it the long summer afternoons in the chalk-pit which had made him dream – or so vividly imagine – the discovery of a real treasure? If it was a dream it was the only dream he remembered from those years, or, if it was a story which he had elaborated at night in bed, it must have been the final effort of a poetic imagination that afterwards had been rigidly controlled. In the various services which had over the years taken him from one part of the world to another, imagination was usually a quality to be suppressed. One's job was to provide facts, to a company (import and export), a newspaper, a government department. Speculation was discouraged. Now the dreaming child was dying of the same disease as the man. He was so different from the child that it was odd to think the child would not outlive him and go on to quite a different destiny.

George said, 'You'll notice some changes, William. When I had the bathroom added, I found I had to disconnect the pipes from the fountain. Something to do with pressure. After all there are no children now to enjoy it.'

'It never played in my time either.'

'I had the tennis-lawn dug up during the war, and it hardly seemed worth while to put it back.'

'I'd forgotten that there *was* a tennis-lawn.'

'Don't you remember it, between the pond and the goldfish tank?'

'The pond? Oh, you mean the lake and the island.'

'Not much of a lake. You could jump on to the island with a short run.'

'I had thought of it as much bigger.'

But all measurements had changed. Only for a dwarf

does the world remain the same size. Even the red-brick wall which separated the garden from the village was lower than he remembered – a mere five feet, but in order to look over it in those days he had always to scramble to the top of some old stumps covered deep with ivy and dusty spiders' webs. There was no sign of these when they drove in: everything was very tidy everywhere, and a handsome piece of ironmongery had taken the place of the swing-gate which they had ruined as children.

'You keep the place up very well,' he said.

'I couldn't manage it without the market-garden. That enables me to put the gardener's wages down as a professional expense. I have a very good accountant.'

He was put into his mother's room with a view of the lawn and the silver birches; George slept in what had been his uncle's. The little bedroom next door which had once been his was now converted into a tiled bathroom – only the prospect was unchanged. He could see the laurel bushes where the Dark Walk began, but they were smaller too. Had the dying horseman found as many changes?

Sitting that night over coffee and brandy, during the long family pauses, Wilditch wondered whether as a child he could possibly have been so secretive as never to have spoken of his dream, his game, whatever it was. In his memory the adventure had lasted for several days. At the end of it he had found his way home in the early morning when everyone was asleep: there had been a dog called Joe who bounded towards him and sent him sprawling in the heavy dew of the lawn. Surely there must have been some basis of fact on which the legend had been built. Perhaps he had run away, perhaps he had been out all night – on the island in the lake or hidden in the Dark Walk – and during those hours he had invented the whole story.

Wilditch took a second glass of brandy and asked tentatively, 'Do you remember much of those summers when we were children here?' He was aware of something unconvincing in the question: the apparently harmless opening gambit of a wartime interrogation.

'I never cared for the place much in those days,' George said surprisingly. 'You were a secretive little bastard.'

'Secretive?'

'And uncooperative. I had a great sense of duty towards you, but you never realized that. In a year or two you were going to follow me to school. I tried to teach you the rudiments of cricket. You weren't interested. God knows what you were interested in.'

'Exploring?' Wilditch suggested, he thought with cunning.

'There wasn't much to explore in fourteen acres. You know, I had such plans for this place when it became mine. A swimming-pool where the tennis-lawn was – it's mainly potatoes now. I meant to drain the pond too – it breeds mosquitoes. Well, I've added two bathrooms and modernized the kitchen, and even that has cost me four acres of pasture. At the back of the house now you can hear the children caterwauling from the council-houses. It's all been a bit of a disappointment.'

'At least I'm glad you haven't drained the lake.'

'My dear chap, why go on calling it a lake? Have a look at it in the morning and you'll see the absurdity. The water's nowhere more than two feet deep.' He added, 'Oh well, the place won't outlive me. My children aren't interested, and the factories are beginning to come out this way. They'll get a reasonably good price for the land – I haven't much else to leave them.' He put some more sugar in his coffee. 'Unless, of course, you'd like to take it on when I am gone?'

'I haven't the money and anyway there's no cause to believe that I won't be dead first.'

'Mother was against my accepting the inheritance,' George said. 'She never liked the place.'

'I thought she loved her summers here.' The great gap between their memories astonished him. They seemed to be talking about different places and different people.

'It was terribly inconvenient, and she was always in trouble with the gardener. You remember Ernest? She said she had to wring every vegetable out of him. (By the way he's still alive, though retired of course – you ought to look him up in the morning. It would please him. He still feels he owns the place.) And then, you know, she always thought it would have been better for us if we could have gone to the seaside. She had an idea that she was robbing us of a heritage – buckets and spades and seawater-bathing. Poor mother, she couldn't afford to turn down Uncle Henry's hospitality. I think in her heart she blamed father for dying when he did without providing for holidays at the sea.'

'Did you talk it over with her in those days?'

'Oh no, not then. Naturally she had to keep a front before the children. But when I inherited the place – you were in Africa – she warned Mary and me about the difficulties. She had very decided views, you know, about any mysteries, and that turned her against the garden. Too much shrubbery, she said. She wanted everything to be very clear. Early Fabian training, I dare say.'

'It's odd. I don't seem to have known her very well.'

'You had a passion for hide-and-seek. She never liked that. Mystery again. She thought it a bit morbid. There was a time when we couldn't find you. You were away for hours.'

'Are you sure it was hours? Not a whole night?'

'I don't remember it at all myself. Mother told me.' They drank their brandy for a while in silence. Then George said, 'She asked Uncle Henry to have the Dark Walk cleared away. She thought it was unhealthy with all the spiders' webs, but he never did anything about it.'

'I'm surprised *you* didn't.'

'Oh, it was on my list, but other things had priority, and now it doesn't seem worth while to make more changes.' He yawned and stretched. 'I'm used to early bed. I hope you don't mind. Breakfast at 8.30?'

'Don't make any changes for me.'

'There's just one thing I forgot to show you. The flush is tricky in your bathroom.'

George led the way upstairs. He said, 'The local plumber didn't do a very good job. Now, when you've pulled this knob, you'll find the flush never quite finishes. You have to do it a second time – sharply like this.'

Wilditch stood at the window looking out. Beyond the Dark Walk and the space where the lake must be, he could see the splinters of light given off by the council-houses; through one gap in the laurels there was even a street-light visible, and he could hear the faint sound of television-sets joining together different programmes like the discordant murmur of a mob.

He said, 'That view would have pleased mother. A lot of the mystery gone.'

'I rather like it this way myself,' George said, 'on a winter's evening. It's a kind of companionship. As one gets older one doesn't want to feel quite alone on a sinking ship. Not being a churchgoer myself . . .' he added, leaving the sentence lying like a torso on its side.

'At least we haven't shocked mother in that way, either of us.'

'Sometimes I wish I'd pleased her, though, about the Dark Walk. And the pond – how she hated that pond too.'

'Why?'

'Perhaps because you liked to hide on the island. Secrecy and mystery again. Wasn't there something you wrote about it once? A story?'

'Me? A story? Surely not.'

'I don't remember the circumstances. I thought – in a school magazine? Yes, I'm sure of it now. She was very angry indeed and she wrote rude remarks in the margin with a blue pencil. I saw them somewhere once. Poor mother.'

George led the way into the bedroom. He said, 'I'm sorry there's no bedside light. It was smashed last week, and I haven't been into town since.'

'It's all right. I don't read in bed.'

'I've got some good detective stories downstairs if you wanted one.'

'Mysteries?'

'Oh, mother never minded those. They came under the heading of puzzles. Because there was always an answer.'

Beside the bed was a small bookcase. He said, 'I brought some of mother's books here when she died and put them in her room. Just the ones that she had liked and no bookseller would take.' Wilditch made out a title, *My Apprenticeship* by Beatrice Webb. 'Sentimental, I suppose, but I didn't want actually to *throw away* her favourite books. Good night.' He repeated, 'I'm sorry about the light.'

'It really doesn't matter.'

George lingered at the door. He said, 'I'm glad to see you here, William. There were times when I thought you were avoiding the place.'

'Why should I?'

'Well, you know how it is. I never go to Harrod's now because I was there with Mary a few days before she died.'

'Nobody has died here. Except Uncle Henry, I suppose.'

'No, of course not. But why did you, suddenly, decide to come?'

'A whim,' Wilditch said.

'I suppose you'll be going abroad again soon?'

'I suppose so.'

'Well, good night.' He closed the door.

Wilditch undressed, and then, because he felt sleep too far away, he sat down on the bed under the poor centre light and looked along the rows of shabby books. He opened Mrs Beatrice Webb at some account of a trade-union congress and put it back. (The foundations of the future Welfare State were being truly and uninterestingly laid.) There were a number of Fabian pamphlets heavily scored with the blue pencil which George had remembered. In one place Mrs Wilditch had detected an error of one decimal point in some statistics dealing with agricultural imports. What passionate concentration must have gone to that discovery. Perhaps because his own life was coming to an end, he thought how little of this, in the almost impossible event of a future, she would have carried with her. A fairy-story in such an event would be a more valuable asset than a Fabian graph, but his mother had not approved of fairy-stories. The only children's book on these shelves was a history of England. Against an enthusiastic account of the battle of Agincourt she had pencilled furiously,

> And what good came of it at last?
> Said little Peterkin.

The fact that his mother had quoted a poem was in itself remarkable.

The storm which he had left behind in London had travelled east in his wake and now overtook him in short gusts of wind and wet that slapped at the pane. He thought, for no reason, It will be a rough night on the island. He had been disappointed to discover from George that the origin of the dream which had travelled with him round the world was probably no more than a story invented for a school magazine and forgotten again, and just as that thought occurred to him, he saw a bound volume called *The Warburian* on the shelf.

He took it out, wondering why his mother had preserved 20 it, and found a page turned down. It was the account of a cricket-match against Lancing and Mrs Wilditch had scored the margin: 'Wilditch One did good work in deep field.' Another turned-down leaf produced a passage under the heading Debating Society: 'Wilditch One spoke succinctly to the motion.' The motion was 'That this House has no belief in the social policies of His Majesty's Government'. So George in those days had been a Fabian too.

He opened the book at random this time and a letter fell out. It had a printed heading, Dean's House, Warbury, and it read, 'Dear Mrs Wilditch, I was sorry to receive your letter of the 3rd and to learn that you were displeased with the little fantasy published by your younger son in *The Warburian.* I think you take a rather extreme view of the tale which strikes me as quite a good imaginative exercise for a boy of thirteen. Obviously he has been influenced by the term's reading of *The Golden Age* – which after all, fanciful though it may be, was written by a governor of the Bank of England.' (Mrs Wilditch had made several blue exclamation marks in the margin – perhaps representing her view of the Bank.) 'Last term's *Treasure Island* too may have contributed. It is always our intention at Warbury to foster the imagination – which I think you rather harshly denigrate when you write of "silly fancies". We have scrupulously kept our side of the bargain, knowing how strongly you feel, and the boy is not "subjected", as you put it, to any religious instruction at all. Quite frankly, Mrs Wilditch, I cannot see any trace of religious feeling in this little fancy – I have read it through a second time before writing to you – indeed the treasure, I'm afraid, is only too material, and quite at the mercy of those "who break in and steal".'

Wilditch tried to find the place from which the letter had fallen, working back from the date of the letter. Eventually he found it: 'The Treasure on the Island' by W.W.

Wilditch began to read.

5

In the middle of the garden there was a great lake and in the middle of the lake an island with a wood. Not everybody knew about the lake, for to reach it you had to find your way down a long dark walk, and not many people's nerves were strong enough to reach the end. Tom knew that he was likely to be undisturbed in that frightening region, and so it was there that he constructed a raft out of old packing cases, and one drear wet day when he knew that everybody would be shut in the house, he dragged the raft to the lake and paddled it across to the island. As far as he knew he was the first to land there for centuries.

It was all overgrown on the island, but from a map he had found in an ancient sea-chest in the attic he made his measurements, three paces north from the tall umbrella pine in the

*middle and then two paces to the right. There seemed to be
nothing but scrub, but he had brought with him a pick and a
spade and with the dint of almost superhuman exertions he
uncovered an iron ring sunk in the grass. At first he thought
it would be impossible to move, but by inserting the point of
the pick and levering it he raised a kind of stone lid and there
below, going into the darkness, was a long narrow passage.*

*Tom had more than the usual share of courage, but even he
would not have ventured further if it had not been for the
parlous state of the family fortunes since his father had died.
His elder brother wanted to go to Oxford but for lack of
money he would probably have to sail before the mast, and
the house itself, of which his mother was passionately fond,
was mortgaged to the hilt to a man in the City called Sir
Silas Dedham whose name did not belie his nature.*

Wilditch nearly gave up reading. He could not reconcile
this childish story with the dream which he remembered.
Only the 'drear wet night' seemed true as the bushes
rustled and dripped and the birches swayed outside. A
writer, so he had always understood, was supposed to
order and enrich the experience which was the source of
his story, but in that case it was plain that the young
Wilditch's talents had not been for literature. He read
with growing irritation, wanting to exclaim again and
again to this thirteen-year-old ancestor of his, 'But why
did you leave that out? Why did you alter this?'

23

The passage opened out into a great cave stacked from floor to ceiling with gold bars and chests overflowing with pieces of eight. There was a jewelled crucifix – Mrs Wilditch had underlined the word in blue – *set with precious stones which had once graced the chapel of a Spanish galleon and on a marble table were goblets of precious metal.*

But, as he remembered, it was an old kitchen-dresser, and there were no pieces of eight, no crucifix, and as for the Spanish galleon . . .

Tom thanked the kindly Providence which had led him first to the map in the attic (but there had been no map. Wilditch wanted to correct the story, page by page, much as his mother had done with her blue pencil) *and then to this rich treasure trove* (his mother had written in the margin, referring to the kindly Providence, 'No trace of religious feeling!!'). *He filled his pockets with the pieces of eight and taking one bar under each arm, he made his way back along the passage. He intended to keep his discovery secret and slowly day by day to transfer the treasure to the cupboard in his room, thus surprising his mother at the end of the holidays with all this sudden wealth. He got safely home unseen by anyone and that night in bed he counted over his new riches while outside it rained and rained. Never had he heard such a storm. It was as though the wicked spirit of his old pirate ancestor raged against him* (Mrs Wilditch had written, 'Eternal punishment I suppose!') *and indeed the* next day, when he returned to the island in the lake, whole *trees had been uprooted and now lay across the entrance to the passage. Worse still there had been a landslide, and now the cavern must lie hidden forever below the waters of the lake. However* (the young Wilditch had added briefly forty years ago) *the treasure already recovered was sufficient to save the family home and send his brother to Oxford.'*

Wilditch undressed and got into bed, then lay on his back listening to the storm. What a trivial conventional day-dream W.W. had constructed – out of what? There had been no attic-room – probably no raft: these were prelimi-naries which did not matter, but why had W.W. so falsified the adventure itself? Where was the man with the beard? The old squawking woman? Of course it had all been a dream, it could have been nothing else but a dream, but a dream too was an experience, the images of a dream had their own integrity, and he felt professional anger at this false report just as his mother had felt at the mistake in the Fabian statistics.

All the same, while he lay there in his mother's bed and thought of her rigid interrogation of W.W.'s story, another theory of the falsifications came to him, perhaps a juster one. He remembered how agents parachuted into France during the bad years after 1940 had been made to memo-rize a cover-story which they could give, in case of torture, with enough truth in it to be checked. Perhaps forty years ago the pressure to tell had been almost as great on W.W.,   25 so that he had been forced to find relief in fantasy. Well, an agent dropped into occupied territory was always given a time-limit after capture. 'Keep the interrogators at bay with silence or lies for just so long, and then you may tell all.' The time-limit had surely been passed in his case a long time ago, his mother was beyond the possibility of hurt, and Wilditch for the first time deliberately indulged his passion to remember.

He got out of bed and, after finding some notepaper stamped, presumably for income-tax purposes, Winton Small Holdings Limited, in the drawer of the desk, he began to write an account of what he had found – or dreamed that he found – under the garden of Winton Hall. The summer night was nosing wetly around the window just as it had done fifty years ago, but, as he wrote, it began to turn grey and recede; the trees of the garden became visible, so that, when he looked up after some hours from his writing, he could see the shape of the broken fountain and what he supposed were the laurels in the Dark Walk, looking like old men humped against the weather.

Part Two

I

Never mind how I came to the island in the lake, never mind whether in fact, as my brother says, it is a shallow pond with water only two feet deep (I suppose a raft can be launched on two feet of water, and certainly I must have always come to the lake by way of the Dark Walk, so that it is not at all unlikely that I built my raft there). Never mind what hour it was — I think it was evening, and I had hidden, as I remember it, in the Dark Walk because George had not got the courage to search for me there. The evening turned to rain, just as it's raining now, and George must have been summoned into the house for shelter. He would have told my mother that he couldn't find me and she must have called from the upstair windows, front and back — perhaps it was the occasion George spoke about tonight. I am not sure of these facts, they are plausible only, I can't yet *see* what I'm describing. But I know that I was not to find George and my mother again for many days ... It cannot, whatever George says, have been less than three days and nights that I spent below the ground. Could he really have forgotten so inexplicable an experience?

And here I am already checking my story as though it 27

were something which had really happened, for what possible relevance has George's memory to the events of a dream?

I dreamed that I crossed the lake, I dreamed . . . that is the only certain fact and I must cling to it, the fact that I dreamed. How my poor mother would grieve if she could know that, even for a moment, I had begun to think of these events as true . . . but, of course, if it were possible for her to know what I am thinking now, there would be no limit to the area of possibility. I dreamed then that I crossed the water (either by swimming – I could already swim at seven years old – or by wading if the lake is really as small as George makes out, or by paddling a raft) and scrambled up the slope of the island. I can remember grass, scrub, brushwood, and at last a wood. I would describe it as a forest if I had not already seen, in the height of the garden-wall, how age diminishes size. I don't remember the umbrella-pine which W.W. described – I suspect he stole the sentinel-tree from *Treasure Island*, but I do know that when I got into the wood I was completely hidden from the house and the trees were close enough together to protect me from the rain. Quite soon I was lost, and yet how could I have been lost if the lake were no bigger than a pond, and the island therefore not much larger than the top of a kitchen-table?

Again I find myself checking my memories as though they were facts. A dream does not take account of size. A puddle can contain a continent, and a clump of trees stretch in sleep to the world's edge. I dreamed, I *dreamed* that I was lost and that night began to fall. I was not frightened. It was as though even at seven I was accustomed to travel. All the rough journeys of the future were already in me then, like a muscle which had only to develop. I curled up among the roots of the trees and slept. When I woke I could still hear the pit-pat of the rain in the upper branches and the steady zing of an insect near by. All these noises come as clearly back to me now as the sound of the rain on the parked cars outside the clinic in Wimpole Street, the music of yesterday.

The moon had risen and I could see more easily around me. I was determined to explore further before the morning came, for then an expedition would certainly be sent in search of me. I knew, from the many books of exploration George had read to me, of the danger to a person lost of walking in circles until eventually he dies of thirst or hunger, so I cut a cross in the bark of the tree (I had brought a knife with me that contained several blades, a small saw and an instrument for removing pebbles from horses' hooves). For the sake of future reference I named the place where I had slept Camp Hope. I had no fear of hunger, for I had apples in both pockets, and as for thirst I had only to continue in a straight line and I would come eventually to the lake again where the water was sweet, or at worst a little brackish. I go into all these details, which

W.W. unaccountably omitted, to test my memory. I had forgotten until now how far or how deeply it extended. Had W.W. forgotten or was he afraid to remember?

I had gone a little more than three hundred yards – I paced the distances and marked every hundred paces or so on a tree – it was the best I could do, without proper surveying instruments, for the map I already planned to draw – when I reached a great oak of apparently enormous age with roots that coiled away above the surface of the ground. (I was reminded of those roots once in Africa where they formed a kind of shrine for a fetish – a seated human figure made out of a gourd and palm fronds and unidentifiable vegetable matter gone rotten in the rains and a great penis of bamboo. Coming on it suddenly, I was frightened, or was it the memory that it brought back which scared me?) Under one of these roots the earth had been disturbed; somebody had shaken a mound of charred tobacco from a pipe and a sequin glistened like a snail in the moist moonlight. I struck a match to examine the ground closer and saw the imprint of a foot in a patch of loose earth – it was pointing at the tree from a few inches away and it was as solitary as the print Crusoe found on the sands of another island. It was as though a one-legged man had taken a leap out of the bushes straight at the tree.

Pirate ancestor! What nonsense W.W. had written, or had he converted the memory of that stark frightening footprint into some comforting thought of the kindly scoundrel, Long John Silver, and his wooden leg?

I stood astride the imprint and stared up the tree, half expecting to see a one-legged man perched like a vulture among the branches. I listened and there was no sound except last night's rain dripping from leaf to leaf. Then – I don't know why – I went down on my knees and peered among the roots. There was no iron ring, but one of the roots formed an arch more than two feet high like the entrance to a cave. I put my head inside and lit another match – I couldn't see the back of the cave.

It's difficult to remember that I was only seven years old. To the self we remain always the same age. I was afraid at first to venture further, but so would any grown man have been, any one of the explorers I thought of as my peers. My brother had been reading aloud to me a month before from a book called *The Romance of Australian Exploration* – my own powers of reading had not advanced quite as far as that, but my memory was green and retentive and I carried in my head all kinds of new images and evocative words – aboriginal, sextant, Murrumbidgee, Stony Desert, and the points of the compass with their big capital letters ESE and NNW had an excitement they have never quite lost. They were like the figure on a watch which at last comes round to pointing the important hour. I was comforted by the thought that Sturt had been sometimes daunted and that Burke's bluster often hid his fear. Now, kneeling by the cave, I remembered a cavern which George Grey, another hero of mine, had entered and how suddenly he had come on the figure of a man ten feet high painted on the wall, clothed from the chin down to the ankles in a red garment. I don't know why, but I was more afraid of that painting than I was of the aborigines who killed Burke, and the fact that the feet and hands which protruded from the garment were said to be badly executed added to the terror. A foot which looked like a foot was only human, but my imagination could play endlessly with the faults of the painter – a club-foot, a claw-foot, the worm-like toes of a bird. Now I associated this strange footprint with the ill-executed painting, and I hesitated a long time before I got the courage to crawl into the cave under the root. Before doing so, in reference to the footprint, I gave the spot the name of Friday's Cave.

2

For some yards I could not even get upon my knees, the roof grated my hair, and it was impossible for me in that position to strike another match. I could only inch along like a worm, making an ideograph in the dust. I didn't notice for a while in the darkness that I was crawling down a long slope, but I could feel on either side of me roots rubbing my shoulders like the banisters of a staircase.

I was creeping through the branches of an underground tree in a mole's world. Then the impediments were passed – I was out the other side; I banged my head again on the earth-wall and found that I could rise to my knees. But I nearly toppled down again, for I had not realized how steeply the ground sloped. I was more than a man's height below ground and, when I struck a match, I could see no finish to the long gradient going down. I cannot help feeling a little proud that I continued on my way, on my knees this time, though I suppose it is arguable whether one can really show courage in a dream.

I was halted again by a turn in the path, and this time I found I could rise to my feet after I had struck another match. The track had flattened out and ran horizontally. The air was stuffy with an odd disagreeable smell like cabbage cooking, and I wanted to go back. I remembered how miners carried canaries with them in cages to test the freshness of the air, and I wished I had thought of bringing our own canary with me which had accompanied us to Winton Hall – it would have been company too in that dark tunnel with its tiny song. There was something, I remembered, called coal-damp which caused explosions, and this passage was certainly damp enough. I must be nearly under the lake by this time, and I thought to myself that, if there was an explosion, the waters of the lake would pour in and drown me.

I blew out my match at the idea, but all the same I

continued on my way in the hope that I might come on an exit a little easier than the long crawl back through the roots of the trees.

Suddenly ahead of me something whistled, only it was less like a whistle than a hiss: it was like the noise a kettle makes when it is on the boil. I thought of snakes and wondered whether some giant serpent had made its nest in the tunnel. There was something fatal to man called a Black Mamba ... I stood stock-still and held my breath, while the whistling went on and on for a long while, before it whined out into nothing. I would have given anything then to have been safe back in bed in the room next to my mother's with the electric-light switch close to my hand and the firm bed-end at my feet. There was a strange clanking sound and a duck-like quack. I couldn't bear the darkness any more and I lit another match, reckless of coal-damp. It shone on a pile of old newspapers and nothing else – it was strange to find I had not been the first person here. I called out 'Hullo!' and my voice went on in diminishing echoes down the long passage. Nobody answered, and when I picked up one of the papers I saw it was no proof of a human presence. It was the *East Anglian Observer* for April 5th 1885 – 'with which is incorporated the *Colchester Guardian*'. It's funny how even the date remains in my mind and the Victorian Gothic type of the titling. There was a faint fishy smell about it as though – oh, eons ago – it had been wrapped

34

around a bit of prehistoric cod. The match burnt my fingers and went out. Perhaps I was the first to come here for all those years, but suppose whoever had brought those papers were lying somewhere dead in the tunnel.

Then I had an idea. I made a torch of the paper in my hand, tucked the others under my arm to serve me later, and with the stronger light advanced more boldly down the passage. After all wild beasts – so George had read to me – and serpents too in all likelihood – were afraid of fire, and my fear of an explosion had been driven out by the greater terror of what I might find in the dark. But it was not a snake or a leopard or a tiger or any other cavern-haunting animal that I saw when I turned the second corner. Scrawled with the simplicity of ancient man upon the left-hand wall of the passage – done with a sharp tool like a chisel – was the outline of a gigantic fish. I held up my paper-torch higher and saw the remains of lettering either half-obliterated or in a language I didn't know.

I was trying to make sense of the symbols when a hoarse voice out of sight called, 'Maria, Maria.'

I stood very still and the newspaper burned down in my hand. 'Is that you, Maria?' the voice said. It sounded to me very angry. 'What kind of a trick are you playing? What's the clock say? Surely it's time for my broth.' And then I heard again that strange quacking sound which I had heard before. There was a long whispering and after that silence.

3

I suppose I was relieved that there were human beings and not wild beasts down the passage, but what kind of human beings could they be except criminals hiding from justice or gypsies who are notorious for stealing children? I was afraid to think what they might do to anyone who discovered their secret. It was also possible, of course, that I had come on the home of some aboriginal tribe . . . I stood there unable to make up my mind whether to go on or to turn back. It was not a problem which my Australian peers could help me to solve, for they had sometimes found the aboriginals friendly folk who gave them fish (I thought of the fish on the wall) and sometimes enemies who attacked with spears. In any case – whether these were criminals or gypsies or aboriginals – I had only a pocket-knife for my defence. I think it showed the true spirit of an explorer that in spite of my fears I thought of the map I must one day draw if I survived and so named this spot Camp Indecision.

My indecision was solved for me. An old woman appeared suddenly and noiselessly around the corner of the passage. She wore an old blue dress which came down to her ankles covered with sequins, and her hair was grey and straggly and she was going bald on top. She was every bit as surprised as I was. She stood there gaping at me and then she opened her mouth and squawked. I learned later that she had no roof to her mouth and was probably saying, 'Who are you?' but then I thought it was some foreign tongue she spoke – perhaps Aborigine – and I replied with an attempt at assurance, 'I'm English.'

The hoarse voice out of sight said, 'Bring him along here, Maria.'

The old woman took a step towards me, but I couldn't bear the thought of being touched by her hands, which were old and curved like a bird's and covered with the brown patches that Ernest, the gardener, had told me were 'grave-marks'; her nails were very long and filled with dirt. Her dress was dirty too and I thought of the sequin I'd seen outside and imagined her scrabbling home through the roots of the tree. I backed up against the side of the passage and somehow squeezed around her. She quacked after me, but I went on. Round a second – or perhaps a third – corner I found myself in a great cave some eight feet high. On what I thought was a throne, but I later realized was an old lavatory-seat, sat a big old man with a white beard yellowing round the mouth from what I suppose now to have been nicotine. He had one good leg, but the right trouser was sewn up and looked stuffed like a bolster. I could see him quite well because an oil-lamp stood on a kitchen-table, beside a carving-knife and two cabbages, and his face came vividly back to me the other day when I was reading Darwin's description of a carrier-pigeon: 'Greatly elongated eyelids, very large external orifices to the nostrils, and a wide gape of mouth.'

He said, 'And who would you be and what are you doing here and why are you burning my newspaper?'

The old woman came squawking around the corner and then stood still behind me, barring my retreat.

I said, 'My name's William Wilditch, and I come from Winton Hall.'

'And where's Winton Hall?' he asked, never stirring from his lavatory-seat.

'Up there,' I said and pointed at the roof of the cave.

'That means precious little,' he said. 'Why, everything is up there, China and all America too and the Sandwich Islands.'

'I suppose so,' I said. There was a kind of reason in most of what he said, as I came to realize later.

'But down here there's only us. We are exclusive,' he said, 'Maria and me.'

I was less frightened of him now. He spoke English. He was a fellow-countryman. I said, 'If you'll tell me the way out I'll be going on my way.'

'What's that you've got under your arm?' he asked me sharply. 'More newspapers?'

'I found them in the passage . . .'

'Finding's not keeping here,' he said, 'whatever it may

be up there in China. You'll soon discover that. Why, that's the last lot of papers Maria brought in. What would we have for reading if we let you go and pinch them?'

'I didn't mean . . .'

'Can you read?' he asked, not listening to my excuses.

'If the words aren't too long.'

'Maria can read, but she can't see very well any more than I can, and she can't articulate much.'

Maria went kwahk, kwahk, behind me, like a bull-frog it seems to me now, and I jumped. If that was how she read I wondered how he could understand a single word. He said, 'Try a piece.'

'What do you mean?'

'Can't you understand plain English? You'll have to work for your supper down here.'

'But it's not supper-time. It's still early in the morning,' I said.

'What o'clock is it, Maria?'

'Kwahk,' she said.

'Six. That's supper-time.'

'But it's six in the morning, not the evening.'

'How do you know? Where's the light? There aren't such things as mornings and evenings here.'

'Then how do you ever wake up?' I asked. His beard shook as he laughed. 'What a shrewd little shaver he is,' he exclaimed. 'Did you hear that, Maria? "How do you ever wake up?" he said. All the same you'll find that life here isn't all beer and skittles and who's your Uncle Joe. If you are clever, you'll learn and if you are not clever . . .' He brooded morosely. 'We are deeper here than any grave was ever dug to bury secrets in. Under the earth or over the earth, it's here you'll find all that matters.' He added angrily, 'Why aren't you reading a piece as I told you to? If you are to stay with us, you've got to jump to it.'

'I don't want to stay.'

'You think you can just take a peek, is that it? and go away. You are wrong – but take all the peek you want and then get on with it.'

I didn't like the way he spoke, but all the same I did as he suggested. There was an old chocolate-stained chest of drawers, a tall kitchen-cupboard, a screen covered with scraps and transfers, and a wooden crate which perhaps served Maria for a chair, and another larger one for a table. There was a cooking-stove with a kettle pushed to one side, steaming yet. That would have caused the whistle I had heard in the passage. I could see no sign of any bed, unless a heap of potato-sacks against the wall served that purpose. There were a lot of breadcrumbs on the earth-floor and a few bones had been swept into a corner as though awaiting interment.

'And now,' he said, 'show your young paces. I've yet to see whether you are worth your keep.'

'But I don't want to be kept,' I said. 'I really don't. It's time I went home.'

'Home's where a man lies down,' he said, 'and this is where you'll lie from now. Now take the first page that comes and read to me. I want to hear the news.'

'But the paper's nearly fifty years old,' I said. 'There's no news in it.'

'News is news however old it is.' I began to notice a way he had of talking in general statements like a lecturer or a prophet. He seemed to be less interested in conversation than in the recital of some articles of belief, odd crazy ones, perhaps, yet somehow I could never put my finger convincingly on an error. 'A cat's a cat even when it's a dead cat. We get rid of it when it's smelly, but news never smells, however long it's dead. News keeps. And it comes round again when you least expect. Like thunder.'

I opened the paper at random and read. 'Garden fête at the Grange. The fête at the Grange, Long Wilson, in aid of Distressed Gentlewomen was opened by Lady (Isobel) Montgomery.' I was a bit put out by the long words coming so quickly, but I acquitted myself with fair credit. He sat on the lavatory-seat with his head sunk a little, listening with attention. 'The Vicar presided at the White Elephant Stall.'

The old man said with satisfaction, 'They are royal beasts.'

'But these were not really elephants,' I said.

'A stall is part of a stable, isn't it? What do you want a

stable for if they aren't real? Go on. Was it a good fate or an evil fate?'

'It's not that kind of fate either,' I said.

'There's no other kind,' he said. 'It's your fate to read to me. It's *her* fate to talk like a frog, and mine to listen because my eyesight's bad. This is an underground fate we suffer from here, and that was a garden fate – but it all comes to the same fate in the end.' It was useless to argue with him and I read on: 'Unfortunately the festivities were brought to an untimely close by a heavy rainstorm.'

Maria gave a kwhak that sounded like a malicious laugh, and 'You see,' the old man said, as though what I had read proved somehow he was right, 'that's fate for you.'

'The evening's events had to be transferred indoors, including the Morris Dancing and the Treasure Hunt.'

'Treasure Hunt?' the old man asked sharply.

'That's what it says here.'

'The impudence of it,' he said. 'The sheer impudence. Maria, did you hear that?'

She kwhahked – this time, I thought, angrily.

'It's time for my broth,' he said with deep gloom, as though he were saying, 'It's time for my death.'

'It happened a long time ago,' I said trying to soothe him.

'Time,' he exclaimed, 'you can — time,' using a word quite unfamiliar to me which I guessed – I don't know

42

how – was one that I could not with safety use myself when I returned home. Maria had gone behind the screen – there must have been other cupboards there, for I heard her opening and shutting doors and clanking pots and pans.

I whispered to him quickly, 'Is she your lubra?'

'Sister, wife, mother, daughter,' he said, 'what difference does it make? Take your choice. She's a woman, isn't she?' He brooded there on the lavatory-seat like a king on a throne. 'There are two sexes,' he said. 'Don't try to make more than two with definitions.' The statement sank into my mind with the same heavy mathematical certainty with which later on at school I learned the rule of Euclid about the sides of an isosceles triangle. There was a long silence.

'I think I'd better be going,' I said, shifting up and down. Maria came in. She carried a dish marked Fido filled with hot broth. Her husband, her brother, whatever he was, nursed it on his lap a long while before he drank it. He seemed to be lost in thought again, and I hesitated to disturb him. All the same, after a while, I tried again.

'They'll be expecting me at home.'

'Home?'

'Yes.'

'You couldn't have a better home than this,' he said. 'You'll see. In a bit of time – a year or two – you'll settle down well enough.'

I tried my best to be polite. 'It's very nice here, I'm sure, but . . .'

'It's no use your being restless. I didn't ask you to come, did I, but now you are here, you'll stay. Maria's a great hand with cabbage. You won't suffer any hardship.'

'But I can't stay. My mother . . .'

'Forget your mother and your father too. If you need anything from up there Maria will fetch it down for you.'

'But I can't stay here.'

'Can't's not a word that you can use to the likes of me.'

'But you haven't any right to keep me . . .'

'And what right had you to come busting in like a thief, getting Maria all disturbed when she was boiling my broth?'

'I couldn't stay here with you. It's not – sanitary.' I don't know how I managed to get that word out. 'I'd die . . .'

'There's no need to talk of dying down here. No one's ever died here, and you've no reason to believe that anyone ever will. We aren't dead, are we, and we've lived a long long time, Maria and me. You don't know how lucky you are. There's treasure here beyond all the riches of Asia. One day, if you don't go disturbing Maria, I'll show you. You know what a millionaire is?' I nodded. 'They aren't one quarter as rich as Maria and me. And they die too, and where's their treasure then? Rockefeller's gone and Fred's gone and Columbus. I sit here and just read about dying – it's an entertainment that's all. You'll find in all those papers what they call an obituary – there's one about a Lady Caroline Winterbottom that made Maria laugh and me. It's summerbottoms we have here, I said, all the year round, sitting by the stove.'

Maria kwahked in the background, and I began to cry more as a way of interrupting him than because I was really frightened.

It's extraordinary how vividly after all these years I can remember that man and the words he spoke. If they were to dig down now on the island below the roots of the tree, I would half expect to find him sitting there still on the old lavatory-seat which seemed to be detached from any pipes or drainage and serve no useful purpose, and yet, if he had really existed, he must have passed his century a long time ago. There was something of a monarch about him and something, as I said, of a prophet and something of the gardener my mother disliked and of a policeman in the next village; his expressions were often countrylike and coarse, but his ideas seemed to move on a deeper level, like roots spreading below a layer of compost. I could sit here now in this room for hours remembering the things he said – I haven't made out the sense of them all yet: they are stored in my memory like a code uncracked which waits for a clue or an inspiration.

He said to me sharply, 'We don't need salt here. There's too much as it is. You taste any bit of earth and you'll find it salt. We live in salt. We are pickled, you might say, in it. Look at Maria's hands, and you'll see the salt in the cracks!'

I stopped crying at once and looked (my attention could always be caught by bits of irrelevant information), and, true enough, there seemed to be grey-white seams running between her knuckles.

'You'll turn salty too in time,' he said encouragingly and drank his broth with a good deal of noise.

I said, 'But I really am going, Mr . . .'

'You can call me Javitt,' he said, 'but only because it's not my real name. You don't believe I'd give you that, do you? And Maria's not Maria – it's just a sound she answers to, you understand me, like Jupiter.'

'No.'

'If you had a dog called Jupiter, you wouldn't believe he was really Jupiter, would you?'

'I've got a dog called Joe.'

'The same applies,' he said and drank his soup. Sometimes I think that in no conversation since have I found the interest I discovered in those inconsequent sentences of his to which I listened during the days (I don't know how many) that I spent below the garden. Because, of course, I didn't leave that day. Javitt had his way.

He might be said to have talked me into staying, though if I had proved obstinate I have no doubt at all that Maria would have blocked my retreat, and certainly I would not have fancied struggling to escape through the musty folds of her clothes. That was the strange balance – to and fro – of those days; half the time I was frightened as though I were caged in a nightmare and half the time I only wanted to laugh freely and happily at the strangeness of his speech and the novelty of his ideas. It was as if, for those hours or days, the only important things in life were two, laughter and fear. (Perhaps the same ambivalence was there when I first began to know a woman.) There are people whose laughter has always a sense of superiority, but it was Javitt who taught me that laughter is more often a sign of equality, of pleasure and not of malice. He sat there on his lavatory seat and he said, 'I shit dead stuff every day, do I? How wrong you are.' (I was already laughing because that was a word I knew to be obscene and I had never heard it spoken before.) 'Everything that comes out of me is alive, I tell you. It's squirming around there, germs and bacilli and the like, and it goes into the ground like a womb, and it comes out somewhere, I dare say, like my daughter did – I forgot I haven't told you about her.'

'Is she here?' I said with a look at the curtain, wondering what monstrous woman would next emerge.

'Oh, no, she went upstairs a long time ago.'

'Perhaps I could take her a message from you,' I said cunningly.

He looked at me with contempt. 'What kind of a

message,' he asked, 'could the likes of you take to the likes of her?' He must have seen the motive behind my offer, for he reverted to the fact of my imprisonment. 'I'm not unreasonable,' he said, 'I'm not one to make hailstorms in harvest time, but if you went back up there you'd talk about me and Maria and the treasure we've got, and people would come digging.'

'I swear I'd say nothing' (and at least I have kept that promise, whatever others I have broken, through all the years until now).

'You talk in your sleep maybe. A boy's never alone. You've got a brother, I dare say, and soon you'll be going to school and hinting of things to make you seem important. There are plenty of ways of keeping an oath and breaking it in the same moment. Do you know what I'd do then? If they came searching? I'd go further in.'

Maria kwahk-kwahked her agreement where she listened from somewhere behind the curtains.

'What do you mean?'

'Give me a hand to get off this seat,' he said. He pressed his hand down on my shoulder and it was like a mountain heaving. I looked at the lavatory-seat and I could see that it had been placed exactly to cover a hole which went down down down out of sight. 'A moit of the treasure's down there already,' he said, 'but I wouldn't let the bastards enjoy what they could find here. There's a little matter of subsidence I've got fixed up so that they'd never see the light of day again.'

'But what would you do below there for food?'

'We've got tins enough for another century or two,' he said. 'You'd be surprised at what Maria's stored away there. We don't use tins up here because there's always broth and cabbage and that's more healthy and keeps the scurvy off, but we've no more teeth to lose and our gums are fallen as it is, so if we had to fall back on tins we would. Why, there's hams and chickens and red salmons' eggs and butter and steak-and-kidney pies and caviar, venison too and marrow-bones, I'm forgetting the fish — cods' roe and sole in white wine, langouste legs, sardines, bloaters, and herrings in tomato-sauce, and all the fruits that ever grew, apples, pears, strawberries, figs, raspberries, plums and greengages and passion fruit, mangoes, grapefruit, loganberries and cherries, mulberries too and sweet things from Japan, not to speak of vegetables, Indian corn and taties, salsify and spinach and that thing they call endive, asparagus, peas and the hearts of bamboo, and I've left out our old friend the tomato.' He lowered himself heavily back on to his seat above the great hole going down.

'You must have enough for two lifetimes,' I said.

'There's means of getting more,' he added darkly, so that I pictured other channels delved through the undersoil of the garden like the section of an ant's nest, and I   49 remembered the sequin on the island and the single footprint.

Perhaps all this talk of food had reminded Maria of her duties because she came quacking out from behind her dusty curtain, carrying two bowls of broth, one medium size for me and one almost as small as an egg-cup for herself. I tried politely to take the small one, but she snatched it away from me.

'You don't have to bother about Maria,' the old man said. 'She's been eating food for more years than you've got weeks. She knows her appetite.'

'What do you cook with?' I asked.

'Calor,' he said.

That was an odd thing about this adventure or rather this dream: fantastic though it was, it kept coming back to ordinary life with simple facts like that. The man could never, if I really thought it out, have existed all those years below the earth, and yet the cooking, as I seem to remember it, was done on a cylinder of Calor-gas.

The broth was quite tasty and I drank it to the end. When I had finished I fidgeted about on the wooden box they had given me for a seat – nature was demanding something for which I was too embarrassed to ask aid.

'What's the matter with you?' Javitt said. 'Chair not comfortable?'

'Oh, it's very comfortable,' I said.

'Perhaps you want to lie down and sleep?'

'No.'

'I'll show you something which will give you dreams,' he said. 'A picture of my daughter.'

'I want to do number one,' I blurted out.

'Oh, is that all?' Javitt said. He called to Maria, who was still clattering around behind the curtain, 'The boy wants to piss. Fetch him the golden po.' Perhaps my eyes showed interest, for he added to me diminishingly, with the wave of a hand, 'It's the least of my treasures.'

All the same it was remarkable enough in my eyes, and I can remember it still, a veritable chamber-pot of gold. Even the young dauphin of France on that long road back from Varennes with his father had only a silver cup at his service. I would have been more embarrassed, doing what I called number one in front of the old man Javitt, if I had not been so impressed by the pot. It lent the everyday affair the importance of a ceremony, almost of a sacrament. I can remember the tinkle in the pot like far-away chimes as though a gold surface resounded differently from china or base metal.

Javitt reached behind him to a shelf stacked with old papers and picked one out. He said, 'Now you look at that and tell me what you think.'

It was a kind of magazine I'd never seen before – full of pictures which are now called cheese-cake. I have no earlier memory of a woman's unclothed body, or as nearly unclothed as made no difference to me then, in the 51 skin-tight black costume. One whole page was given up to a Miss Ramsgate, shot from all angles. She was the favourite contestant for something called Miss England and might later go on, if she were successful, to compete for the title of Miss Europe, Miss World and after that Miss Universe. I stared at her as though I wanted to memorize her for ever. And that is exactly what I did.

'That's our daughter,' Javitt said.

'And did she become . . .'

'She was launched,' he said with pride and mystery, as though he were speaking of some moon-rocket which had at last after many disappointments risen from the pad and soared to outer space. I looked at the photograph, at the wise eyes and the inexplicable body, and I thought, with all the ignorance children have of age and generations, I never want to marry anybody but her. Maria put her hand through the curtains and quacked, and I thought, she would be my mother then, but not a hoot did I care. With that girl for my wife I could take anything, even school and growing up and life. And perhaps I could have taken them, if I had ever succeeded in finding her.

Again my thoughts were interrupted. For if I am remembering a vivid dream – and dreams do stay in all their detail far longer than we realize – how would I have known at that age about such absurdities as beauty-contests? A dream can only contain what one has experienced, or, if you have sufficient faith in Jung, what our ancestors have experienced. But Calor-gas and the Ramsgate Beauty Queen . . .? They are not ancestral memories, nor the memories of a child of seven. Certainly my mother did not allow us to buy with our meagre pocket-money – sixpence a week? – such papers as that. And yet the image is there, caught once and for all, not only the expression of the eyes, but the expression of the body too, the particular tilt of the breasts, the shallow scoop of the navel like something carved in sand, the little trim buttocks – the dividing line swung between them close and regular like the single sweep of a pencil. Can a child of seven fall in love for life with a body? And there is a further mystery which did not occur to me then: how could a couple as old as Javitt and Maria have had a daughter so young in the period when such contests were the vogue?

'She's a beauty,' Javitt said, 'you'll never see her like where your folks live. Things grow differently underground, like a mole's coat. I ask you where there's softness softer than that?' I'm not sure whether he was referring to the skin of his daughter or the coat of a mole.

I sat on the golden po and looked at the photograph and listened to Javitt as I would have listened to my own father if I had possessed one. His sayings are fixed in my memory like the photograph. Gross some of them seem now, but they did not appear gross to me then when even the graffiti on walls were innocent. Except when he called me 'boy' or 'snapper' or something of the kind he seemed 53 unaware of my age: it was not that he talked to me as an equal but as someone from miles away, looking down from his old lavatory-seat to my golden po, from so far away that he couldn't distinguish my age, or perhaps he was so old that anyone under a century or so seemed much alike to him. All that I write here was not said at that moment. There must have been many days or nights of conversation – you couldn't down there tell the difference – and now I dredge the sentences up, in no particular order, just as they come to mind, sitting at my mother's desk so many years later.

4

'You laugh at Maria and me. You think we look ugly. I tell you she could have been painted if she had chosen by some of the greatest – there's one that painted women with three eyes – she'd have suited him. But she knew how to tunnel in the earth like me, when to appear and when not to appear. It's a long time now that we've been alone down here. It gets more dangerous all the time – if you can speak of time – on the upper floor. But don't think it hasn't happened before. But when I remember . . .' But what he remembered has gone from my head, except only his concluding phrase and a sense of desolation: 'Looking round at all those palaces and towers, you'd have thought they'd been made like a child's castle of the desert-sand.

'In the beginning you had a name only the man or woman knew who pulled you out of your mother. Then there was a name for the tribe to call you by. That was of little account, but of more account all the same than the name you had with strangers; and there was a name used in the family – by your pa and ma if it's those terms you call them by nowadays. The only name without any power at all was the name you used to strangers. That's why I call myself Javitt to you, but the name the man who pulled me out knew – that was so secret I had to keep him as a friend for life, so that he wouldn't even tell me because of the responsibility it would bring – I might let it slip before a stranger. Up where you come from they've begun to forget the power of the name. I wouldn't be surprised if you only had the one name and what's the good of a name everyone knows? Do you suppose even I feel secure here with my treasure and all – because, you see, as it turned out, I got to know the first name of all. He told it me before he died, before I could stop him, with a hand over his mouth. I doubt if there's anyone in the world except me who knows his first name. It's an awful temptation to speak it out loud – introduce it casually into the conversation like you might say by Jove, by George, for Christ's sake. Or whisper it when I think no one's attentive.

'When I was born, time had a different pace to what it has now. Now you walk from one wall to another, and it takes you twenty steps – or twenty miles – who cares? – between the towns. But when I was young we took a leisurely way. Don't bother me with "I must be gone now" or "I've been away so long". I can't talk to you in terms of time – your time and my time are different. Javitt isn't my usual name either even with strangers. It's one I thought up fresh for you, so that you'll have no power at all. I'll change it right away if you escape. I warn you that.

'You get a sense of what I mean when you make love with a girl. The time isn't measured by clocks. Time is fast or slow or it stops for a while altogether. One minute is different to every other minute. When you make love it's a pulse in a man's part which measures time and when you spill yourself there's no time at all. That's how time comes and goes, not by an alarm-clock made by a man with a magnifying glass in his eye. Haven't you ever heard them say, "It's – time" up there?' and he used again the word which I guessed was forbidden like his name, perhaps because it had power too.

'I dare say you are wondering how Maria and me could make a beautiful girl like that one. That's an illusion people have about beauty. Beauty doesn't come from beauty. All that beauty can produce is prettiness. Have

56 you never looked around upstairs and counted the beauti-

ful women with their pretty daughters? Beauty diminishes all the time, it's the law of diminishing returns, and only when you get back to zero, to the real ugly base of things, there's a chance to start again free and independent. Painters who paint what they call ugly things know that. I can still see that little head with its cap of blonde hair coming out from between Maria's thighs and how she leapt out of Maria in a spasm (there wasn't any doctor down here or midwife to give her a name and rob her of power – and she's Miss Ramsgate to you and to the whole world upstairs). Ugliness and beauty; you see it in war too; when there's nothing left of a house but a couple of pillars against the sky, the beauty of it starts all over again like before the builder ruined it. Perhaps when Maria and I go up there next, there'll only be pillars left, sticking up around the flattened world like it was fucking time.' (The word had become a familiar to me by this time and no longer had the power to shock.)

'Do you know, boy, that when they make those maps of the universe you are looking at the map of something that looked like that six thousand million years ago? You can't be much more out of date than that, I'll swear. Why, if they've got pictures up there of us taken yesterday, they'll see the world all covered with ice – if their photos are a bit more up to date than ours, that is. Otherwise we won't be there at all, maybe, and it might just as well be a photo of the future. To catch a star while it's alive you have to be as nippy as if you were snatching at a racehorse as it goes by.

'You are a bit scared still of Maria and me because you've never seen anyone like us before. And you'd be scared to see our daughter too, there's no other like her in whatever country she's in now, and what good would a scared man be to her? Do you know what a rogue-plant is? And do you know that white cats with blue eyes are deaf? People who keep nursery-gardens look around all the time at the seedlings and they throw away any oddities like weeds. They call them rogues. You won't find many white cats with blue eyes and that's the reason. But sometimes you find someone who wants things different, who's tired of all the plus signs and wants to find zero, and he starts breeding away with the differences. Maria and I are both rogues and we are born of generations of rogues. Do you think I lost this leg in an accident? I was born that way just like Maria with her squawk. Generations of us uglier and uglier, and suddenly out of Maria comes our daughter, who's Miss Ramsgate to you. I don't speak her name even when I'm asleep. We're unique like the Red Grouse. You ask anybody if they can tell you where the Red Grouse came from.

'You are still wondering why we are unique. It's because for generations we haven't been thrown away. Man kills or throws away what he doesn't want. Somebody once in Greece kept the wrong child and exposed the right one, and then one rogue at least was safe and it only needed another. Why, in Tierra del Fuego in starvation years they kill and eat their old women because the dogs are of more value. It's the hardest thing in the world for a rogue to survive. For hundreds of years now we've been living underground and we'll have the laugh of you yet, coming up above for keeps in a dead world. Except I'll bet you your golden po that Miss Ramsgate will be there somewhere – her beauty's rogue too. We have long lives, we – Javitts to you. We've kept our ugliness all those years and why shouldn't she keep her beauty? Like a cat does. A cat is as beautiful the last day as the first. And it keeps its spittle. Not like a dog.

'I can see your eye light up whenever I say Miss Ramsgate, and you still wonder how it comes Maria and I have a child like that in spite of all I'm telling you. Elephants go on breeding till they are ninety years old, don't they, and do you suppose a rogue like Javitt (which isn't my real name) can't go on longer than a beast so stupid it lets itself be harnessed and draw logs? There's another thing we have in common with elephants. No one sees us dead.

'We know the sex-taste of female birds better than we know the sex-taste of women. Only the most beautiful in the hen's eyes survives, so when you admire a peacock you know you have the same taste as a pea-hen. But women are more mysterious than birds. You've heard of beauty and the beast, haven't you? They have rogue-tastes. Just look at me and my leg. You won't find Miss Ramsgate by going round the world preening yourself like a peacock to attract a beautiful woman – she's our daughter and she had rogue-tastes too. She isn't for someone who wants a beautiful wife at his dinner-table to satisfy his vanity, and an understanding wife in bed who'll treat him just the same number of times as he was accustomed to at school – so many times a day or week. She went away, our daughter did, with a want looking for a want – and not a want you can measure in inches either or calculate in numbers by the week. They say that in the northern countries people make love for their health, so it won't be any good looking for her in the north. You might have to go as far as Africa or China. And talking of China . . .'

5

Sometimes I think that I learned more from Javitt – this man who never existed – than from all my schoolmasters. He talked to me while I sat there on the po or lay upon the sacks as no one had ever done before or has ever done since. I could not have expected my mother to take time away from the Fabian pamphlets to say, 'Men are like monkeys – they don't have any season in love, and the monkeys aren't worried by this notion of dying. They tell us from pulpits we're immortal and then they try to frighten us with death. I'm more a monkey than a man. To the monkeys death's an accident. The gorillas don't bury their dead with hearses and crowns of flowers, thinking one day it's going to happen to them and they better put on a show if they want one for themselves too. If one of them dies, it's a special case, and so they can leave it in the ditch. I feel like them. But I'm not a special case yet. I keep clear of hackney-carriages and railway-trains, you won't find horses, wild dogs or machinery down here. I love life and I survive. Up there they talk about natural death, but it's natural death that's unnatural. If we lived for a thousand years – and there's no reason we shouldn't – there'd always be a smash, a bomb, tripping over your left foot – those are the natural deaths. All we need to live is a bit of effort, but nature sows booby-traps in our way.

'Do you believe those skulls monks have in their cells are set there for contemplation? Not on your life. They don't believe in death any more than I do. The skulls are there for the same reason you'll see a queen's portrait in an embassy – they're just part of the official furniture. Do you believe an ambassador ever looks at that face on the wall with a diamond tiara and an empty smile?

'Be disloyal. It's your duty to the human race. The human race needs to survive and it's the loyal man who dies first from anxiety or a bullet or overwork. If you have 61 to earn a living, boy, and the price they make you pay is loyalty, be a double agent – and never let either of the two sides know your real name. The same applies to women and God. They both respect a man they don't own, and they'll go on raising the price they are willing to offer. Didn't Christ say that very thing? Was the prodigal son loyal or the lost shilling or the strayed sheep? The obedient flock didn't give the shepherd any satisfaction or the loyal son interest his father.

'People are afraid of bringing May blossom into the house. They say it's unlucky. The real reason is it smells strong of sex and they are afraid of sex. Why aren't they afraid of fish then, you may rightly ask? Because when they smell fish they smell a holiday ahead and they feel safe from breeding for a short while.'

I remember Javitt's words far more clearly than the passage of time; certainly I must have slept at least twice on the bed of sacks, but I cannot remember Javitt sleeping until the very end – perhaps he slept like a horse or a god, upright. And the broth – that came at regular intervals, so far as I could tell, though there was no sign anywhere of a clock, and once I think they opened for me a tin of sardines from their store (it had a very Victorian label on it of two bearded sailors and a seal, but the sardines tasted good).

I think Javitt was glad to have me there. Surely he
could not have been talking quite so amply over the years

to Maria who could only quack in response, and several times he made me read to him from one of the newspapers. The nearest to our time I ever found was a local account of the celebrations for the relief of Mafeking. ('Riots,' Javitt said, 'purge like a dose of salts.')

Once he told me to pick up the oil-lamp and we would go for a walk together, and I was able to see how agile he could be on his one leg. When he stood upright he looked like a rough carving from a tree-trunk where the sculptor had not bothered to separate the legs, or perhaps, as with the image on the cave, they were 'badly executed'. He put one hand on each wall and hopped gigantically in front of me, and when he paused to speak (like many old people he seemed unable to speak and move at the same time) he seemed to be propping up the whole passage with his arms as thick as pit-beams. At one point he paused to tell me that we were now directly under the lake. 'How many tons of water lie up there?' he asked me – I had never thought of water in tons before that, only in gallons, but he had the exact figure ready, I can't remember it now. Further on, where the passage sloped upwards, he paused again and said, 'Listen,' and I heard a kind of rumbling that passed overhead and after that a rattling as little cakes of mud fell around us. 'That's a motor-car,' he said, as an explorer might have said, 'That's an elephant.'

I asked him whether perhaps there was a way out near there since we were so close to the surface, and he made   63 his answer, even to that direct question, ambiguous and general like a proverb. 'A wise man has only one door to his house,' he said.

What a boring old man he would have been to an adult mind, but a child has a hunger to learn which makes him sometimes hang on the lips of the dullest schoolmaster. I thought I was learning about the world and the universe from Javitt, and still to this day I wonder how it was that a child could have invented these details, or have they accumulated year by year, like coral, in the sea of the unconscious around the original dream?

There were times when he was in a bad humour for no apparent reason, or at any rate for no adequate reason. An example: for all his freedom of speech and range of thought, I found there were tiny rules which had to be obeyed, else the thunder of his invective broke – the way I had to arrange the spoon in the empty broth-bowl, the method of folding a newspaper after it had been read, even the arrangement of my limbs on the bed of sacks.

'I'll cut you off,' he cried once and I pictured him lopping off one of my legs to resemble him. 'I'll starve you, I'll set you alight like a candle for a warning. Haven't I given you a kingdom here of all the treasures of the earth and all the fruits of it, tin by tin, where time can't get in to destroy you and there's no day or night, and you go and defy me with a spoon laid down longways in a saucer? You come of an ungrateful generation.' His arms waved about and cast shadows like wolves on the wall behind the oil-lamp, while Maria sat squatting behind a cylinder of Calor-gas in an attitude of terror.

'I haven't even seen your wonderful treasure,' I said with feeble defiance.

'Nor you won't,' he said, 'nor any lawbreaker like you. You lay last night on your back grunting like a small swine, but did I curse you as you deserved? Javitt's patient. He forgives and he forgives seventy times seven, but then you go and lay your spoon longways . . .' He gave a great sigh like a wave withdrawing. He said, 'I forgive even that. There's no fool like an old fool and you will search a long way before you find anything as old as I am – even among the tortoises, the parrots and the elephants. One day I'll show you the treasure, but not now. I'm not in the right mood now. Let time pass. Let time heal.'

I had found the way, however, on an earlier occasion to set him in a good humour and that was to talk to him about his daughter. It came quite easily to me, for I found myself to be passionately in love, as perhaps one can only be at an age when all one wants is to give and the thought of taking is very far removed. I asked him whether he was sad when she left him to go 'upstairs' as he liked to put it.

'I knew it had to come,' he said. 'It was for that she was born. One day she'll be back and the three of us will be together for keeps.'

'Perhaps I'll see her then,' I said.

'You won't live to see that day,' he said, as though it was I who was the old man, not he.

'Do you think she's married?' I asked anxiously.

'She isn't the kind to marry,' he said. 'Didn't I tell you she's a rogue like Maria and me? She has her roots down here. No one marries who has his roots down here.'

'I thought Maria and you were married,' I said anxiously.

He gave a sharp crunching laugh like a nut-cracker closing. 'There's no marrying in the ground,' he said. 'Where would you find the witnesses? Marriage is public. Maria and me, we just grew into each other, that's all, and then she sprouted.'

I sat silent for a long while, brooding on that vegetable picture. Then I said with all the firmness I could muster, 'I'm going to find her when I get out of here.'

'If you get out of here,' he said, 'you'd have to live a very long time and travel a very long way to find her.'

'I'll do just that,' I replied.

He looked at me with a trace of humour. 'You'll have to take a look at Africa,' he said, 'and Asia – and then there's America, North and South, and Australia – you might leave out the Arctic and the other Pole – she was always a warm girl.' And it occurs to me now when I think of the life I have led since, that I have been in most of those regions – except Australia where I have only twice touched down between planes.

'I will go to them all,' I said, 'and I'll find her.' It was as though the purpose of life had suddenly come to me as it must have come often enough to some future explorer when he noticed on a map for the first time an empty space in the heart of a continent.

'You'll need a lot of money,' Javitt jeered at me.

'I'll work my passage,' I said, 'before the mast.' Perhaps it was a reflection of that intention which made the young author W. W. menace his elder brother with such a fate before preserving him for Oxford of all places. The mast was to be a career sacred to me – it was not for George.

'It'll take a long time,' Javitt warned me.

'I'm young,' I said.

I don't know why it is that when I think of this conversation with Javitt the doctor's voice comes back to me saying hopelessly, 'There's always hope.' There's hope perhaps, but there isn't so much time left now as there was then to fulfil a destiny.

That night, when I lay down on the sacks, I had the impression that Javitt had begun to take a favourable view of my case. I woke once in the night and saw him sitting there on what is popularly called a throne, watching me. He closed one eye in a wink and it was like a star going out.

Next morning after my bowl of broth, he suddenly

spoke up. 'Today,' he said, 'you are going to see my
treasure.'

6

It was a day heavy with the sense of something fateful
coming nearer – I call it a day but for all I could have told
down there it might have been a night. And I can only
compare it in my later experience with those slow hours I
have sometimes experienced before I have gone to meet a
woman with whom for the first time the act of love is
likely to come about. The fuse has been lit, and who can
tell the extent of the explosion? A few cups broken or a
house in ruins?

For hours Javitt made no further reference to the
subject, but after the second cup of broth (or was it
perhaps, on that occasion, the tin of sardines?) Maria
disappeared behind the screen and when she reappeared
she wore a hat. Once, years ago perhaps, it had been a
grand hat, a hat for the races, a great black straw affair;
now it was full of holes like a colander decorated with one
drooping scarlet flower which had been stitched and re-
stitched and stitched again. I wondered when I saw her
dressed like that whether we were about to go 'upstairs'.
But we made no move. Instead she put a kettle upon the
68   stove, warmed a pot and dropped in two spoonfuls of tea.

Then she and Javitt sat and watched the kettle like a couple of soothsayers bent over the steaming entrails of a kid, waiting for a revelation. The kettle gave a thin preliminary whine and Javitt nodded and the tea was made. He alone took a cup, sipping it slowly, with his eyes on me, as though he were considering and perhaps revising his decision.

On the edge of his cup, I remember, was a tea-leaf. He took it on his nail and placed it on the back of my hand. I knew very well what that meant. A hard stalk of tea indicated a man upon the way and the soft leaf a woman; this was a soft leaf. I began to strike it with the palm of my other hand counting as I did so, 'One, two, three.' It lay flat, adhering to my hand. 'Four, five.' It was on my fingers now and I said, triumphantly, 'In five days,' thinking of Javitt's daughter in the world above.

Javitt shook his head. 'You don't count time like that with us,' he said. 'That's five decades of years.' I accepted his correction – he must know his own country best, and it's only now that I find myself calculating, if every day down there were ten years long, what age in our reckoning could Javitt have claimed?

I have no idea what he had learned from the ceremony of the tea, but at least he seemed satisfied. He rose on his one leg, and now that he had his arms stretched out to either wall, he reminded me of a gigantic crucifix, and the crucifix moved in great hops down the way we had taken 69 the day before. Maria gave me a little push from behind and I followed. The oil-lamp in Maria's hand cast long shadows ahead of us.

First we came under the lake and I remembered the tons of water hanging over us like a frozen falls, and after that we reached the spot where we had halted before, and again a car went rumbling past on the road above. But this time we continued our shuffling march. I calculated that now we had crossed the road which led to Winton Halt; we must be somewhere under the inn called The Three Keys, which was kept by our gardener's uncle, and after that we should have arrived below the Long Mead, a field with a small minnowy stream along its northern border owned by a farmer called Howell. I had not given up all idea of escape and I noted our route carefully and the distance we had gone. I had hoped for some side-passage which might indicate that there was another entrance to the tunnel, but there seemed to be none and I was disappointed to find that, before we travelled below the inn, we descended quite steeply, perhaps in order to avoid the cellars – indeed at one moment I heard a groaning and a turbulence as though the gardener's uncle were taking delivery of some new barrels of beer.

We must have gone nearly half a mile before the passage came to an end in a kind of egg-shaped hall. Facing us was a kitchen-dresser of unstained wood, very similar to the one in which my mother kept her stores of jam, sultanas, raisins and the like.

'Open up Maria,' Javitt said, and Maria shuffled by me, clanking a bunch of keys and quacking with excitement, while the lamp swung to and fro like a censer.

'She's heated up,' Javitt said. 'It's many days since she saw the treasure last.' I do not know which kind of time he was referring to then, but judging from her excitement I think the days must really have represented decades – she had even forgotten which key fitted the lock and she tried them all and failed and tried again before the tumbler turned.

I was disappointed when I first saw the interior – I had expected gold bricks and a flow of Maria Theresa dollars spilling on the floor, and there were only a lot of shabby cardboard-boxes on the upper shelves and the lower shelves were empty. I think Javitt noted my disappointment and was stung by it. 'I told you,' he said, 'the moit's down below for safety.' But I wasn't to stay disappointed very long. He took down one of the biggest boxes off the top shelf and shook the contents on to the earth at my feet, as though defying me to belittle *that*.

And *that* was a sparkling mass of jewellery such as I had never seen before – I was going to say in all the colours of the rainbow, but the colours of stones have not that pale girlish simplicity. There were reds almost as deep as raw liver, stormy blues, greens like the underside of a wave, yellow sunset colours, greys like a shadow on snow, and stones without colour at all that sparkled brighter than all the rest. I say I'd seen nothing like it: it is the scepticism of middle age which leads me now to compare that treasure trove with the caskets overflowing with artificial jewellery which you sometimes see in the shop-windows of Italian tourist-resorts.

And there again I find myself adjusting a dream to the kind of criticism I ought to reserve for some agent's report on the import or export value of coloured glass. If this was a dream, these were real stones. Absolute reality belongs to dreams and not to life. The gold of dreams is not the diluted gold of even the best goldsmith, there are no diamonds in dreams made of paste – what seems is. 'Who seems most kingly is the king.'

I went down on my knees and bathed my hands in the treasure and while I knelt there Javitt opened box after box and poured the contents upon the ground. There is no avarice in a child. I didn't concern myself with the value of this horde: it was simply a treasure, and a treasure is to be valued for its own sake and not for what it will buy. It was only years later, after a deal of literature and learning and knowledge at second hand, that W.W. wrote of the treasure as something with which he could save the family fortunes. I was nearer to the jackdaw in my dream, caring only for the glitter and the sparkle.

'It's nothing to what lies below out of sight,' Javitt remarked with pride.

There were necklaces and bracelets, lockets and bangles, pins and rings and pendants and buttons. There were quantities of those little gold objects which girls like to hang on their bracelets: the Vendôme column and the Eiffel Tower and a Lion of St Mark's, a Champagne bottle and a tiny booklet with leaves of gold inscribed with the names of places important perhaps to a pair of lovers – Paris, Brighton, Rome, Assisi and Moreton-in-Marsh. There were gold coins too – some with the heads of Roman emperors and others of Victoria and George IV and Frederick Barbarossa. There were birds made out of precious stone with diamond-eyes, and buckles for shoes and belts, hairpins too with the rubies turned into roses, and vinaigrettes. There were toothpicks of gold, and swizzlesticks, and little spoons to dig the wax out of your ears of gold too, and cigarette-holders studded with diamonds, and small boxes of gold for pastilles and snuff, horseshoes for the ties of hunting men, and emerald-hounds for the lapels of hunting women: fishes were there too and little carrots of ruby for luck, diamond-stars which had perhaps decorated generals or statesmen, golden key-rings with emerald-initials, and sea-shells picked out with pearls, and a portrait of a dancing-girl in gold and enamel, with Haidee inscribed in what I suppose were rubies.

'Enough's enough,' Javitt said, and I had to drag myself

away, as it seemed to me, from all the riches in the world, its pursuits and enjoyments. Maria would have packed everything that lay there back into the cardboard-boxes, but Javitt said with his lordliest voice, 'Let them lie,' and back we went in silence the way we had come, in the same order, our shadows going ahead. It was as if the sight of the treasure had exhausted me. I lay down on the sacks without waiting for my broth and fell asleep at once. In my dream within a dream somebody laughed and wept.

7

I have said that I can't remember how many days and nights I spent below the garden. The number of times I slept is really no guide, for I slept simply when I had the inclination or when Javitt commanded me to lie down, there being no light or darkness save what the oil-lamp determined, but I am almost sure it was after this sleep of exhaustion that I woke with the full intention somehow to reach home again. Up till now I had acquiesced in my captivity with little complaint; perhaps the meals of broth were palling on me, though I doubt if that was the reason, for I have fed for longer, with as little variety and less appetite, in Africa; perhaps the sight of Javitt's treasure had been a climax which robbed my story of any further interest; perhaps, and I think this is the most likely reason, I wanted to begin my search for Miss Ramsgate.

Whatever the motive, I came awake determined from my deep sleep, as suddenly as I had fallen into it. The wick was burning low in the oil-lamp and I could hardly distinguish Javitt's features and Maria was out of sight somewhere behind the curtain. To my astonishment Javitt's eyes were closed – it had never occurred to me before that there were moments when these two might sleep. Very quietly, with my eyes on Javitt, I slipped off my shoes – it was now or never. When I had got them off with less sound than a mouse makes, an idea came to me and I withdrew the laces – I can still hear the sharp ting of the metal tag ringing on the gold po beside my sacks. I thought I had been too clever by half, for Javitt stirred – but then he was still again and I slipped off my makeshift bed and crawled over to him where he sat on the lavatory-seat. I knew that, unfamiliar as I was with the tunnel, I could never outpace Javitt, but I was taken aback when I realized that it was impossible to bind together the ankles of a one-legged man.

But neither could a one-legged man travel without the help of his hands – the hands which lay now conveniently folded like a statue's on his lap. One of the things my brother had taught me was to make a slip-knot. I made one now with the laces joined and very gently, millimetre by millimetre, passed it over Javitt's hands and wrists, then pulled it tight.

I had expected him to wake with a howl of rage and even in my fear felt some of the pride Jack must have experienced at outwitting the giant. I was ready to flee at once, taking the lamp with me, but his very silence detained me. He only opened one eye, so that again I had the impression that he was winking at me. He tried to move his hands, felt the knot, and then acquiesced in their imprisonment. I expected him to call for Maria, but he did nothing of the kind, watching me with his one open eye.

Suddenly I felt ashamed of myself. 'I'm sorry,' I said.

'Ha, ha,' he said, 'my prodigal, the strayed sheep, you're learning fast.'

'I promise not to tell a soul.'

'They wouldn't believe you if you did,' he said.

'I'll be going now,' I whispered with regret, lingering there absurdly, as though with half of myself I would have been content to stay for always.

'You better,' he said. 'Maria might have different views from me.' He tried his hands again. 'You tie a good knot.'

'I'm going to find your daughter,' I said, 'whatever you may think.'

'Good luck to you then,' Javitt said. 'You'll have to travel a long way; you'll have to forget all your school-masters try to teach you; you must lie like a horse-trader and not be tied up with loyalties any more than you are here, and who knows? I doubt it, but you might, you just might.'

I turned away to take the lamp, and then he spoke again. 'Take your golden po as a souvenir,' he said. 'Tell them you found it in an old cupboard. You've got to have something when you start a search to give you substance.'

'Thank you,' I said, 'I will. You've been very kind.' I began – absurdly in view of his bound wrists – to hold out my hand like a departing guest; then I stooped to pick up the po just as Maria, woken perhaps by our voices, came through the curtain. She took the situation in as quick as a breath and squawked at me – what I don't know – and made a dive with her bird-like hand.

I had the start of her down the passage and the advantage of the light, and I was a few feet ahead when I reached Camp Indecision, but at that point, what with the wind of my passage and the failing wick, the lamp went out. I dropped it on the earth and groped on in the dark. I could hear the scratch and whimper of Maria's sequin dress, and my nerves leapt when her feet set the lamp rolling on my tracks. I don't remember much after that. Soon I was crawling upwards, making better speed on my knees than she could do in her skirt, and a little later I saw a grey light where the roots of the tree parted. When I came up into the open it was much the same early morning hour as the one when I had entered the cave. I could hear kwahk, kwahk, kwahk, come up from below the ground – I don't know if it was a curse or a menace or just a farewell, but for many nights afterwards I lay in bed afraid that the door would open and Maria would come in to fetch me, when the house was silent and asleep. Yet strangely enough I felt no fear of Javitt, then or later.

Perhaps – I can't remember – I dropped the gold po at the entrance of the tunnel as a propitiation to Maria; certainly I didn't have it with me when I rafted across the lake or when Joe, our dog, came leaping out of the house at me and sent me sprawling on my back in the dew of the lawn by the green broken fountain.

Part Three

I

Wilditch stopped writing and looked up from the paper. The night had passed and with it the rain and the wet wind. Out of the window he could see thin rivers of blue sky winding between the banks of cloud, and the sun as it slanted in gleamed weakly on the cap of his pen. He read the last sentence which he had written and saw how again at the end of his account he had described his adventure as though it were one which had really happened and not something that he had dreamed during the course of a night's truancy or invented a few years later for the school-magazine. Somebody, early though it was, trundled a wheelbarrow down the gravel-path beyond the fountain. The sound, like the dream, belonged to childhood.

He went downstairs and unlocked the front door. There unchanged was the broken fountain and the path which led to the Dark Walk, and he was hardly surprised when he saw Ernest, his uncle's gardener, coming towards him behind the wheelbarrow. Ernest must have been a young man in the days of the dream and he was an old man now, but to a child a man in the twenties approaches middle-age and so he seemed much as Wilditch remembered him.

There was something of Javitt about him, though he had a big moustache and not a beard – perhaps it was only a brooding and scrutinizing look and that air of authority and possession which had angered Mrs Wilditch when she approached him for vegetables.

'Why, Ernest,' Wilditch said, 'I thought you had retired?'

Ernest put down the handle of the wheelbarrow and regarded Wilditch with reserve. 'It's Master William, isn't it?'

'Yes. George said –'

'Master George was right in a way, but I have to lend a hand still. There's things in this garden others don't know about.' Perhaps he *had* been the model for Javitt, for there was something in his way of speech that suggested the same ambiguity.

'Such as . . .?'

'It's not everyone can grow asparagus in chalky soil,' he said, making a general statement out of the particular in the same way Javitt had done. 'You've been away a long time, Master William.'

'I've travelled a lot.'

'We heard one time you was in Africa and another time in Chinese parts. Do you like a black skin, Master William?'

'I suppose at one time or another I've been fond of a black skin.'

'I wouldn't have thought they'd win a beauty prize,' Ernest said.

'Do you know Ramsgate, Ernest?'

'A gardener travels far enough in a day's work,' he said. The wheelbarrow was full of fallen leaves after the night's storm. 'Are the Chinese as yellow as people say?'

'No.'

There *was* a difference, Wilditch thought: Javitt never asked for information, he gave it: the weight of water, the age of the earth, the sexual habits of a monkey. 'Are there many changes in the garden,' he asked, 'since I was here?'

'You'll have heard the pasture was sold?'

'Yes. I was thinking of taking a walk before breakfast – down the Dark Walk perhaps to the lake and the island.'

'Ah.'

'Did you ever hear any story of a tunnel under the lake?'

'There's no tunnel there. For what would there be a tunnel?'

'No reason that I know. I suppose it was something I dreamed.'

'As a boy you was always fond of that island. Used to hide there from the missus.'

'Do you remember a time when I ran away?'

'You was always running away. The missus used to tell me to and find you. I'd say to her right out, straight as I'm talking to you, I've got enough to do digging the 81 potatoes you are always asking for. I've never known a woman get through potatoes like she did. You'd have thought she ate them. She could have been living on potatoes and not on the fat of the land.'

'Do you think I was treasure-hunting? Boys do.'

'You was hunting for something. That's what I said to the folk round here when you were away in those savage parts – not even coming back here for your uncle's funeral. "You take my word," I said to them, "he hasn't changed, he's off hunting for something, like he always did, though I doubt if he knows what he's after," I said to them. "The next we hear," I said, "he'll be standing on his head in Australia."'

Wilditch remarked with regret, 'Somehow I never looked there'; he was surprised that he had spoken aloud. 'And The Three Keys, is it still in existence?'

'Oh, it's there all right, but the brewers bought it when my uncle died and it's not a free house any more.'

'Did they alter it much?'

'You'd hardly know it was the same house with all the pipes and tubes. They put in what they call pressure, so you can't get an honest bit of beer without a bubble in it. My uncle was content to go down to the cellar for a barrel, but it's all machinery now.'

'When they made all those changes you didn't hear any talk of a tunnel under the cellar?'

'Tunnel again. What's got you thinking of tunnels? The

only tunnel I know is the railway tunnel at Bugham and that's five miles off.'

'Well, I'll be walking on, Ernest, or it will be breakfast time before I've seen the garden.'

'And I suppose now you'll be off again to foreign parts. What's it to be this time? Australia?'

'It's too late for Australia now.'

Ernest shook his brindled head at Wilditch with an air of sober disapproval. 'When I was born,' he said, 'time had a different pace to what it seems to have now,' and, lifting the handle of the wheelbarrow, he was on his way towards the new iron gate before Wilditch had time to realize he had used almost the very words of Javitt. The world was the world he knew.

2

The Dark Walk was small and not very dark – perhaps the laurels had thinned with the passing of time, but the cobwebs were there as in his childhood to brush his face as he went by. At the end of the walk there was the wooden gate on to the green which had always in his day been locked – he had never known why that route out of the garden was forbidden him, but he had discovered a way of opening the gate with the rim of a halfpenny. Now he could find no halfpennies in his pocket.

When he saw the lake he realized how right George had been. It was only a small pond, and a few feet from the margin there was an island the size of the room in which last night they had dined. There *were* a few bushes growing there, and even a few trees, one taller and larger than the others, but certainly it was neither the sentinel-pine of W. W.'s story nor the great oak of his memory. He took a few steps back from the margin of the pond and jumped.

He hadn't quite made the island, but the water in which he landed was only a few inches deep. Was any of the water deep enough to float a raft? He doubted it. He sloshed ashore, the water not even penetrating his shoes. So this little spot of earth had contained Camp Hope and Friday's Cave. He wished that he had the cynicism to laugh at the half-expectation which had brought him to the island.

The bushes came only to his waist and he easily pushed through them towards the largest tree. It was difficult to believe that even a small child could have been lost here. He was in the world that George saw every day, making his round of a not very remarkable garden. For perhaps a minute, as he pushed his way through the bushes, it seemed to him that his whole life had been wasted, much as a man who has been betrayed by a woman wipes out of his mind even the happy years with her. If it had not been for his dream of the tunnel and the bearded man and the hidden treasure, couldn't he have made a less restless life for himself, as George in fact had done, with marriage, children, a home? He tried to persuade himself that he was exaggerating the importance of a dream. His lot had probably been decided months before that when George was reading him *The Romance of Australian Exploration*. If a child's experience does really form his future life, surely he had been formed, not by Javitt, but by Grey and Burke. It was his pride that at least he had never taken his various professions seriously: he had been loyal to no one – not even to the girl in Africa (Javitt would have approved his disloyalty). Now he stood beside the ignoble tree that had no roots above the ground which could possibly have formed the entrance to a cave and he looked back at the house: it was so close that he could see George at the window of the bathroom lathering his face. Soon the bell would be going for breakfast and they would be sitting opposite each other exchanging the morning small talk. There was a good train back to London at 10.25. He supposed that it was the effect of his disease that he was so tired – not sleepy but achingly tired as though at the end of a long journey.

After he had pushed his way a few feet through the bushes he came on the blackened remains of an oak; it had been split by lightning probably and then sawed close to the ground for logs. It could easily have been the source of his dream. He tripped on the old roots hidden in the 85 grass, and squatting down on the ground he laid his ear close to the earth. He had an absurd desire to hear from somewhere far below the kwahk, kwahk from a roofless mouth and the deep rumbling of Javitt's voice saying, 'We are hairless, you and I,' shaking his beard at him, 'so's the hippopotamus and the elephant and the dugong – you wouldn't know, I suppose, what a dugong is. We survive the longest, the hairless ones.'

But, of course, he could hear nothing except the emptiness you hear when a telephone rings in an empty house. Something tickled his ear, and he almost hoped to find a sequin which had survived the years under the grass, but it was only an ant staggering with a load towards its tunnel.

Wilditch got to his feet. As he levered himself upright, his hand was scraped by the sharp rim of some metal object in the earth. He kicked the object free and found it was an old tin chamber-pot. It had lost all colour in the ground except that inside the handle there adhered a few flakes of yellow paint.

3

How long he had been sitting there with the pot between his knees he could not tell; the house was out of sight: he was as small now as he had been then – he couldn't see over the tops of the bushes, and he was back in Javitt's time. He turned the pot over and over; it was certainly not a golden po, but that proved nothing either way; a child might have mistaken it for one when it was newly painted. Had he then really dropped this in his flight – which meant that somewhere underneath him now Javitt sat on his lavatory-seat and Maria quacked beside the Calorgas . . .? There was no certainty; perhaps years ago, when the paint was fresh, he had discovered the pot, just as he had done this day, and founded a whole afternoon legend around it. Then why had W.W. omitted it from his story?

Wilditch shook the loose earth out of the po, and it rang on a pebble just as it had rung against the tag of his shoelace fifty years ago. He had a sense that there was a decision he had to make all over again. Curiosity was growing inside him like the cancer. Across the pond the bell rang for breakfast and he thought, 'Poor mother – she had reason to fear,' turning the tin chamber-pot on his lap.

PENGUIN 60s
are published on the occasion of Penguin's 60th anniversary

FOR THE BEST IN PAPERBACKS, LOOK FOR THE

In every corner of the world, on every subject under the sun, Penguin represents quality and variety—the very best in publishing today.

For complete information about books available from Penguin—including Puffins, Penguin Classics, and Arkana—and how to order them, write to us at the appropriate address below. Please note that for copyright reasons the selection of books varies from country to country.
